The Sheriff's Sweetheart

Cheryl Wright

1

Contents

From the Author

He's been gone more than 18 years now, but I'll never forget the rodeos my dad (and mother) took us to as kids. We looked forward to going each and every year.

Born in the country (as we kids were), my dad was a country man through and through. His first ever job was at a rodeo. He went on to become a ranger, and a horse breaker, amongst other things. His brother looked after horses all his working life, including taking tourists on trail rides. Every now and then I managed to insinuate myself into those trips.

I grew up with horses, and the country ways of doing things. And I'm so glad I did.

Sadly, we moved to the city down the track, but I loved (and still love) horses so much, I spent nearly all my extra money and most of my weekends going on horse rides.

Thanks to my very dear friends (and authors), Margaret Tanner and Susan Horsnell.

Without their encouragement, this book would not be written.

Thanks also to Alan, my husband of 43 years, who has been a relentless supporter of my

writing for as long as I can remember.

Disclaimer

This book is a work of fiction.

Any resemblance to persons, living or dead, or places, events or locales is purely coincidental.

The characters and towns contained within are productions of the author's imagination and are used fictitiously.

Although facts are found throughout, the author has embellished or changed some for the sake of the story.

Chapter One

Isabella O'Reilly stared out the dusty bus window.

She was tired after the long trip from Wyoming and felt disheveled. She was even a little nervous about her visit.

It had been nearly six months since she'd been a bridesmaid in her cousin Missy's wedding in the tiny town of River Valley, Montana.

Six months of pining for Chase Callahan, Missy's new brother-in-law.

She remembered the feel of his arms around her while they danced after the ceremony, and the emptiness when the music stopped and they'd returned to their seats.

The warmth of his arms made her feel protected. She'd felt safe in his arms. She'd wanted to stay there in his arms.

Forever.

As they'd danced the bridal waltz, he'd looked down at her with such hunger in his eyes, and she was certain he was going to kiss her.

He'd leaned forward, his lips close to hers. So close she could feel his warm breath. His beautiful brown eyes searched hers, waiting for her acceptance. Or denial.

She'd licked her lips, and moved closer to Chase, and then.... the music stopped.

She suddenly felt cheated and bereft as he dropped his arms and escorted her back to the bridal table, his hand to the small of her back.

She shook her head to clear the memories away.

Isabella had spent these past months thinking about Chase and trying to get him out of her head. It was affecting her work, and she'd even been injured a couple of times. At least that's what she'd told everyone.

Missy suggested she needed a break, and invited her to High Calibre, her husband Rory's ranch.

If she was truthful with herself, Isabella would admit she really came to see Chase, not Missy.

* * *

Sheriff Chase Callahan sat in his office scratching his head.

His concentration hadn't been the same since his brother's wedding. His mind had been 100% on the job back then. He'd managed to track down the killer who had stalked Rory's now-wife, and had arrested him, with Missy's help.

The pair were blissfully happy, and he was pleased for them. Rory hadn't been happy for a very long time, throwing himself into his work as a way to feel complete. Only it hadn't worked.

And then Missy came along.

Up until that point, he and his brothers had tried everything to get Rory away from the ranch, and out into the community, where he had a chance to meet someone who might be his soul-mate.

But he had rebelled against their efforts, until finally they'd worn him down. He eventually went to the Bar and Grill to have a meal and see the new entertainment. That entertainment was Missy, and he'd saved her butt from an obnoxious, drunken cowboy. That was the beginning of their friendship, which quickly moved to the next level. That ultimately led to their small wedding on Rory's ranch.

Chase had clicked with Missy's cousin Isabella at the wedding, and had nearly kissed her, but the moment had been lost.

Just as well, because as it turned out, she lived in another state, and he knew from experience, long distance relationships didn't work.

He sighed and went back to his paperwork.

* * *

Missy stood impatiently at the bus stop, waiting the arrival of her closest cousin, Isabella.

They'd practically grown up together, living in close proximity to each other. They even went to the same school, then eventually worked in the same rodeo.

She squealed as the bus rounded the corner. She would have jumped up and down too if she'd hasn't been carrying an extra passenger in her belly. She rubbed her hands across her precious cargo and smiled. Rory had been ecstatic at the news. A new little Callahan to expand the family.

Someone has to do it, he'd said with a grin.

The bus pulled up in front of Missy, and she stood watching for Isabella to emerge. Only she didn't.

Missy didn't know what to think. Her cousin had messaged her to say she was on the bus, so Missy knew she hadn't missed it.

The driver was already handing luggage to the other passengers when a disheveled passenger emerged. She struggled down the steps, one of her wrists in plaster, the other carrying a small bag.

"Oh my God!" Missy shouted as she ran forward to help her cousin. "What happened? Did you have another fall?" Missy was distraught at Isabella's appearance.

As she took the hand luggage, Isabella wrapped her arms around Missy and cried. The two women held each other for what seemed an eternity.

They were interrupted when the driver wanted to hand over the luggage so he could be on his way.

After securing the luggage, they were strapped securely in Missy's car and were soon on their way. "Want to talk about it?" she asked Isabella.

Her cousin shook her head, so Missy left her alone. For now.

* * *

Isabella's silence spoke more than words.

Her cousin had told Missy she'd taken a few tumbles lately, but this was unexpected.

Not only was Isabella injured, but she was almost unrecognisable. She'd lost so much weight, and her clothes were practically falling off her. She was thin before, but now she was waif-like.

Missy glanced across as she drove to High Calibre. She reached out and put her hand on Isabella's knee. "Are you okay?" she asked.

The other woman nodded. "I'll be better after a shower and some clean clothes." She licked her lips, and Missy was certain she was on the verge of tears. "I've had one too many falls," she said. "I'm thinking of giving it up."

Missy's head turned sharply. "Really?" Isabella had been in the rodeo business way too long, and Missy was certain she'd stay there forever.

"So far this season I've broken my clavicle, humerus, and now my wrist," she almost whispered. "Enough is enough."

"I know," Missy said. "I've been quite worried about you. I can't say I'll be sorry if you give it away."

Isabella didn't answer – just sat in silence as they continued their journey.

* * *

It was meant to be his day off, but instead, Chase was at the office, deep in paperwork.

He was a hands-on sheriff, which meant he spent most of his time out in the field. As a result, paperwork had to take a back-seat, and was always the last thing to be done.

He had nothing better to do, so his weekends were filled with catching up.

He was up to his ears in useless waste-of-time bureaucratic rubbish when his cell rang.

"Callahan." Chase didn't mince words. Didn't see the point.

It was his brother Rory, inviting him over for lunch. When Chase declined, Rory insisted, cryptically telling him it was in his best interest.

Curious, Chase accepted.

Truth be told, he was annoyed for the intrusion into his usual Sunday routine. But he was also pleased for the break.

* * *

Chase removed his black cowboy hat as he entered his brother's ranch house.

Their mother had been a stickler for hats off in the house, and it had stuck with all the boys, right into adulthood.

He hung it on the hook inside the door where everyone was expected to leave their hats.

The kitchen was empty, so he headed for the sitting room where he could hear the faint sound of voices.

"Hello," he called, letting them know he'd arrived.

As he entered the sitting room, Isabella stood, and stared at him. A slow smile came to her face, and he smiled back.

She took a few steps toward him, and he met her halfway. "Chase," she said quietly, as her voice hitched in her throat.

Apparently he was as much a surprise to her, as she was to him.

As he strode toward her, he looked her up and down, noticing the massive weight loss. That's when he saw it.

11

The plaster on her arm.

As they met in the middle of the room, his arms went up around her. She felt so good. He could stand like this for hours, and not regret even one second of it.

He vividly remembered the last time he'd held her in his arms. The way she'd felt, so soft and pliable, and definitely all woman.

But now she was just skin and bone. Chase was worried for her. What had she done to herself?

If he was truly honest with himself, he had to admit he'd pined for her since she'd left. He felt guilt at not trying to contact her before this. He winced as he though about his dead wife, Jenny, and what she might think.

Despite himself, he knew Isabella was special to him. "I missed you. A lot," he whispered in her ear as he pulled her closer.

* * *

Isabella revelled in Chase's arms. This was exactly where she wanted to be. Where she should be.

When he whispered in her ear, his warm breath almost had her undone. In his arms was exactly where she wanted to be, needed to be, but was it the best thing for Chase?

When she'd left after the wedding, she knew she'd made a mistake.

Instead of going back home all those months ago, she should have stayed in River Valley.

There was nothing stopping her. Except maybe her job, and she could have easily ditched that. If she had, perhaps she wouldn't be in the position she was in right now.

She had thought about Chase day and night. It was excruciating knowing he was a confirmed bachelor, and knowing he wasn't interested in a relationship. Or getting hitched, as he called it, so she'd decided to move on.

It was the worst decision of her life.

* * *

It had been an enjoyable lunch, and an enjoyable afternoon.

Missy sat them together for lunch. Not that Chase was complaining – he wasn't. He was right where he wanted to be. Close to Isabella.

Apart from her appearance, she seemed the same as she was at the wedding.

But the more she spoke, the more he noticed it. She was no longer the outgoing bubbly Isabella he'd met earlier in the year.

"Tell me about your job," he'd said, curious how she could be injured earning a living.

Knowing Missy and many of her friends had worked in the rodeo, nothing would surprise him.

13

"My job is to prepare the bulls to be ridden," she said, glancing down into her lap.

"And you've been injured how many times?"

She glared at him. "I'm not one of your damned criminals, you know."

Everyone stopped talking at once, and the silence was palpable.

He ran his fingers through his hair and stared into her face. "Of course you're not," he said. "I'm just concerned for you."

"Well don't be," she snapped. "Anyway, I'm on indefinite leave until I work out what I want to do." She stood and retreated to her room where she sat and cried until she was spent.

Isabella had no idea what she would do next. Her biggest concern right now was whether or not Chase would see through her façade.

* * *

I don't know what is going on, but something definitely is," Missy told Chase. "She's so thin, she looks ill." She rung her hands in her lap. "I'm really worried about her."

"Me too," Chase interjected. "All those injuries..."

Missy's head snapped up. "She's done that job for nearly ten years without a single injury. All of

14

a sudden she has three broken bones in as many months?" She looked at Chase with worried eyes.

"I'm not buying it," she said. "Something else is going on."

"I know she's your cousin," Chase said. "But how well do you really know Isabella?"

"We grew up together," Missy told him. "We've always been close. We went to school together, worked together," she added. "We even dated some of the same boys in high school."

"But that woman who was just here?" Her eyes filled with fear. "That woman I don't know," she said quietly.

Rory leaned over and put his arms around her, pulling her into a big bear hug.

"Leave it with me," Chase said. "I'll get to the bottom of it."

He stood, reached for his hat, and was quickly gone. A man on a mission.

After Chase left, Missy went to Isabella's room and quietly tapped on the door. "Isabella?" She stopped and listened. Perhaps she was asleep?

But it was far from late, and Missy thought perhaps she just wanted to be left alone. She was certain she was right, but persisted anyway.

"Isabella," she called softly. "Open the door. I just want to make sure you're alright."

The door slowly opened, and Isabella peeked around the door, eyes red and puffy.

She left the door ajar, and went to sit on the bed.

Missy sat beside her, not saying a word. Instead she hugged her friend tightly, and rubbed her hands up her back.

Isabella quietly sobbed on Missy's shoulder.

When she was spent, Missy spoke quietly. "I know something is going on," she said. "I don't know what it is, but I'm hoping you will tell me."

Isabella shook her head. "I-I'm alright," she said. "I'm just stressed – after my long trip."

Missy knew that was a lie, but didn't say so. She stared into Isabella's face, hoping she would give up at least some information. But no, she stayed quiet. And determined.

"Well then," Missy said, realizing she was fighting a losing battle. "Why don't we get you cleaned up, and go sit outside and watch the sun set when it's time." It was more a statement than a question, and she was determined in her quest.

If Isabella didn't want to talk, so be it, but she couldn't sit in her room and wallow in her thoughts.

Missy would have missed the small nod if she hadn't been staring at her cousin.

As they walked toward the bathroom, Isabella let out an errant sob. Missy pulled her close and hugged her again.

She took a clean face washer from the linen press, and ran some cold water into the basin, then left Isabella to her own devices.

"I'll meet you on the porch," she said, as she left the room.

Missy poured three cool drinks and took them outside where Rory already sat, taking in the beautiful view ahead of them.

"She's not talking," she told her husband. "And that's not a good sign. Isabella has always been very open with me." She wiped an errant tear from her cheek, and Rory pulled her close.

"It will be alright, darlin'," he said. "Chase is on the case."

After what seemed like forever, Isabella joined them. "Beautiful sunset," she said, sitting down and accepting her drink.

Missy knew they had a difficult task ahead of them, but for Isabella's sake, they had to find out what was going on.

* * *

Rory sat across from his brother as he spoke on the phone.

"Yes. No. Is that so?" He stared intently at Rory as he listened to the person on the other end of the call.

"And she didn't....." His face turned angry. "I thank you for being so honest. You have a good day, Sir." He slammed the receiver into its cradle and sat silently for several minutes, his face getting redder the longer he sat.

Rory dare not say a word. He knew his brother well and could see he needed to calm down.

Chase pulled off his black cowboy hat, ran his fingers through his blond hair, then ran them across his stubbled chin. "Damn it!"

He shouted so loudly and so suddenly that Rory almost fell out of his chair.

Rory watched him closely. This was not a good sign.

A variety of expressions crossed Chase's face.

"So, what did you find out, Bro?" Rory tried to keep his expression blank but was sure he'd failed. "Are you even going to give me a hint?"

He knew from the get-go this was a case Chase didn't want. Knew he didn't want to investigate Isabella. He was very fond of her. Maybe more fond than Chase wanted to admit, even to his brother.

Chase suddenly stood and headed out of his office without a word, his hand raised to stop Rory from speaking.

"Dinner tonight?" Rory asked to his retreating back.

He was obviously mad as hell and stormed off without another word. Rory knew better than to push him while he was in that frame of mind.

Chapter Two

Isabella sat in her room, quietly contemplating.

She'd been here nearly a week now, but no one had mentioned her injuries again. Strange. She had an appointment today to have her plaster removed. It would be a blessed relief.

There was a tap on the door. "It's me, Missy." She only just heard the quiet voice through the door. "Can I come in?"

For a minute Isabella thought about not answering. Pretending she wasn't there, but Missy would know she was. She opened the door.

Missy smiled at her. "So... today is the big day. Plaster off. I'll bet that will be a big relief." She sat next to Isabella on the unmade bed.

Isabella knew it should be made by now. Even with a plaster on her arm, it was very doable. She was in a bad place psychologically and needed to shake herself out of it. But knew it wasn't as simple as it seemed.

Depression was not that easy to get rid of.

"You look so sad," Missy told her. "I wish I could just hug your sadness away." She reached over and hugged her cousin tightly.

Isabella felt tears roll down her cheeks, despite her determination to stay strong. Perhaps that was part of her problem? She hadn't shared her situation with anyone. Didn't want anyone else tied up in her struggles. And she certainly didn't want them placed in danger.

No, she would deal with it in her own way.

* * *

Chase sat at his sheriff's desk, mulling over the situation in his mind.

This was a difficult case, made harder by the fact he was personally involved.

A little light bulb went off in his head. He needed someone else to take over this investigation. He would get one of his deputies to look into the case on his behalf.

In the meantime, he had decided to keep his distance from Isabella. That meant not visiting Rory and his lovely wife, Missy.

He just wasn't sure he could keep his mouth shut when it came to interacting with Isabella right now. She hadn't exactly lied to him, but hadn't told the truth either.

It absolutely appalled him that she could do that – right to his face. But on some level, he understood why she had.

He reached over to the intercom and spoke to his secretary. "Call Deputy Chris Dolan in here please Sarah," he said rather abruptly.

Chase knew he was testy, but couldn't help it. What he'd learned had put him in a foul mood.

He fiddled about with objects on his desk, and had tried to do paperwork, but nothing worked. He was annoyed and frustrated all at the same time.

He needed to get to the bottom of this, and quickly.

Was Isabella in imminent danger? He closed his eyes. He did his best thinking that way. There were four Callahan brothers, and they were all capable of protecting her. They *would* protect her, no matter what.

He knew they would without even asking.

They were Callahan's – cowboys from way back, and cowboys always protected their lady folk. That's exactly what they would do in this instance.

A knock at the door interrupted his thoughts. "Enter!" He didn't mean to shout, but that's how it came out.

"You wanted to see me, Sheriff?" Outside of work, Chris called him Chase, but he insisted on formalities when they were on duty.

Chase waved him in. "Sit." He sighed deeply, and Deputy Dolan studied him. He was out of character and he knew it.

"I have a personal problem," he explained. "Well, it's not really a personal problem, it's...." He was rambling, he knew he was.

Chris removed his cowboy hat and scratched his head. "Are you alright, Sheriff?" He looked concerned for his superior. The last time Chase remembered behaving this way was after his wife Jenny was killed in a car accident some years back. Chris was around when that had happened, so knew the sheriff and his moods well.

He sighed deeply and stared at Chris for several minutes. "No," he said. "No, I'm not. A dear friend is in trouble, and I need you to get to the bottom of it."

Chris looked relieved. "Of course," he said. "Tell me what you need."

* * *

Missy drove Isabella to the doctor's office to have her plaster removed.

It was half an hour's drive to the nearest doctor, but it gave them a chance to talk. Unfortunately, Isabella wasn't really in a talkative mood, so Missy prompted her.

"I'll bet my last dollar you'll be glad to have that plaster off," Missy said, taking her eyes from the road for only seconds.

Isabella wriggled her fingers on her plastered hand. "Sure will," she said then sighed. "After six weeks, you get over it. I can't wait to have a long, hot bath."

Missy reached over and touched Isabella on the knee. "Then you shall have one. Tonight." Her cousin deserved a bit of pampering. A thought suddenly popped into her head. "Here's a thought – why don't we invite Grace over, and have a girl's night in?"

Grace was Jordon's new wife. Jordon being another Callahan brother. Being a veterinarian, he could have removed Isabella's plaster, but felt it better a 'human' doctor did the honors. After all, he'd said, Isabella may need further treatment that he couldn't provide.

For the first time in days, Isabella smiled. "I'd like that," she said. "It will be nice to spend some time with Grace as well." The three women had all worked at the same rodeo for many years, so were all old friends, as well as Missy and Isabella being cousins.

"It's a date then!" Missy was ecstatic. It was the first time for ages she'd managed to get any sort of enthusiasm from Isabella.

Isabella screwed up her face. "I'm probably not going to be able to do face masks like I usually do on these nights," she said, distressed that she couldn't do something she loved.

Missy waved her hand in the air as though brushing the thought away. "Don't stress on it. We'll have a movie night. But we'll probably do more talking that watching."

She turned to Isabella and smiled, and Isabella felt more relaxed than she'd been in months.

"Popcorn?"

"Of course," Missy said. "What's a movie night without popcorn?"

"You've Got Mail?" Isabella said hopefully. "It's my favorite. Has been forever."

Suddenly Isabella felt deflated. "What about Rory?" she asked. We'll be kicking him out of his own space."

Missy reached over and touched her on the knee. "Rory will not mind. I promise. I'll send him over to Chase's place, and they can have a boy's night in. Jordon will probably join them since Grace will be with us."

Isabella was relieved. "And Kody too?" Kody was another brother but was more unsociable than the others, if that was possible.

Missy shrugged her shoulders. "Who knows. He's like a silent partner. Rarely ever heard from, despite repeated attempts." Missy locked eyes with Isabella as they pulled into the doctor's car park. "He's not unlike Chase really. They both distance themselves from everyone else. I think it's a natural reaction to loneliness," Missy told her.

Isabella bowed her head and looked into her lap. She was lonely too. And she dearly wanted to spend more time with Chase, but she wasn't so sure Chase was interested in spending time with her.

* * *

"You cannot begin to image the relief of having that cast off."

After the two women got into the car for the return trip home, Isabella slumped into the seat. "The doctor said I have to do physical therapy," Isabella said. "Is that a problem? Because if it is..."

"Of course not," Missy interrupted. "It gives me a chance to leave the house more, and maybe," she stared across at Isabella. "Just maybe we can have some shopping days. Buy clothes, get coffee, just spend time together."

She reached over and hugged her cousin tight. "God knows you need a break."

Isabella held onto Missy like she was never going to let go. "Thank you," she whispered, then leaned back into her seat.

Missy stared at her face. She looked so ragged, her face was drawn, and she rarely smiled. She was a shadow of the real Isabella, and it made Missy incredibly sad.

Rory said his brother Chase was "looking into things" but that's all he said. Truth be told, Rory didn't know. Chase kept his cards close to his chest most of the time, and she was sure this time would be no different.

Chase would treat Isabella's situation like a regular case. Even if it was out of his jurisdiction.

Missy knew he would be doing all he could and felt relieved because of it. She leaned back in the seat and turned on the ignition.

"I don't know about you, but I'm not ready to go home. Let's go have coffee." She slowly drove out of the car park, and headed back to River Valley, where they would go to Aunt Lizzie's Kitchen – the local café.

Isabella sat back and closed her eyes, not opening them again until they arrived at Aunt Lizzy's. Missy didn't know if she was tired, or whether Isabella was assuring she wasn't asked any questions.

* * *

"This is my cousin, Isabella." Aunt Lizzie reached out and shook Isabella's hand, and smiled.

"Nice to meet you, Isabella," she said, then turned to Missy. "Which brother are we hooking this lovely lady up with?" She chucked and seemed surprised at Missy's answer.

"Isabella and Chase hooked up on our wedding day," Missy said.

Aunt Lizzie squealed. "Oh my, that is amazing news!" She sat down at the table and took

27

Isabella's hand. "I'm so happy for you both. That man deserves happiness, after all he's been through." She smiled, her overwhelming joy evident.

Tears began to well in her eyes, and Missy reached out and put her hand on Aunt Lizzie's shoulder. "It might be a little early to get so carried away," she said. "Chase has been a little distant lately. We haven't seen him for several days."

The older woman jumped up out of her chair. "That just won't do," she said. She sat down again and put her head in her hands. "I've got it," she said enthusiastically. "Do you ladies have any plans for this afternoon after you leave here?"

Isabella looked to Missy who shook her head.

"Leave it with me." With that, Aunt Lizzie stood once more and walked away, a gleam in her eye.

* * *

The two cousins walked toward the exit of Aunt Lizzie's Kitchen, and Missy pulled out her wallet to pay the bill.

After she handed over the cash for their drinks, Lizzie told them to wait a minute.

She returned with a tray holding a large coffee, and a slice of homemade carrot cake. "This is for Chase," she said, a huge grin on her face.

"But we won't see him," Missy protested.

28

Lizzie chuckled. "No, you won't," she said, laughing. "But Isabella will. You can send her in the right direction, and she will do the rest." She turned to Isabella. "Tell Chase it's a gift from Aunt Lizzie."

The older woman turned and walked away, not allowing further protest.

Missy smiled at the other woman's devious intent, then headed out the door. She took Isabella to the Sheriff's Office a couple of blocks down the street, then sent her inside – alone.

Isabella gingerly walked through the main door of the Sheriff's Office.

She felt a little bewildered. After all she was being sent here alone, on a fool's mission. Chase had seemed distant when they'd met up last. He was no longer interested in her, she was certain.

As she walked further into the building she came across a receptionist standing at the counter.

"Can I help you?"

"I want to see the sheriff," she said quietly, not sure her request would be granted. After all, who was she to him?

The receptionist looked her up and down, and took in the coffee and cake. "I'm guessing this is not police business," the woman said with a smile, curiosity more than anything else written all over her face.

Isabella shook her head. "I'm a friend," she said softly, not sure she could really call herself a friend. "Isabella," she added, as she went to sit down.

She watched as the receptionist made a call, almost whispering into the phone. She grinned at Isabella. "He'll be out soon." She then returned to what she was doing before.

Isabella didn't have to wait long until Chase arrived in the reception area, almost running toward her. He grabbed her by the shoulders and stared into her eyes. "Are you okay?" The look on his face almost scared her.

She gazed into his mesmerizing brown eyes and pushed the coffee and cake toward him. "A, a gift from Aunt Lizzie." She held the tray out in front of her.

He grinned. "That conniving....." He didn't finish the sentence but took the tray and walked Isabella toward his office, his relief clearly evident.

He looked back over his shoulder at his grinning receptionist. "I'm not taking calls, thanks Sally."

Once inside, he closed the door. Putting the tray of proffered goods on his desk, he silently wrapped Isabella in his arms.

He held her tight, and Isabella savoured the feel of him. Loved having him so close. She just stood for several moments, not sure what to do, but finally wrapped her arms around him.

She moved in closer and rested her head against his shoulder. "I've missed you, Chase," she said, so quietly he could easily have missed it.

"I've missed you too, Isabella," he said, tightening his grip on her.

She looked up at him.

He leaned forward and kissed her forehead, his lips lingering.

"Isabella..." His words were breathless, and her heart beat rapidly. She felt weak, knowing this man she felt drawn to reciprocated her feelings.

"Chase," she said, equally breathless. Without warning, his lips covered hers, and she was lost. She could stay like this with Chase forever, but knew it was not going to happen. She would have to move on before it was too late. She couldn't run the risk of him being caught up in this situation.

Wouldn't allow that to happen.

Chapter Three

Chase stood with his arms encasing Isabella. He could stand like this for eternity. Stand with *her* forever.

He hadn't thought about another woman since Jenny had died so suddenly. So tragically. Hadn't dated, hadn't wanted to.

But since he'd met Isabella, all that changed.

He felt a twinge of guilt.

He still loved Jenny, was still in love with her. Was sure he always would be.

They'd been married a relatively short time when she'd been killed in a tragic accident.

He'd blamed himself for a very long time, but knew in his heart it wasn't his fault. He couldn't predict the actions of a drunk driver, any more than he could predict someone being run over a by a bus, or hit by a train.

It was just one of those things. Tragic. Heartbreaking. But not a damned thing he could do about it.

Jenny wouldn't begrudge him happiness, he was certain of it. And Isabella certainly made him happy. There was a pull there. A certain buzz between them.

When he held her, he felt like he'd come home. Like things would be okay again.

Yet he knew things were not okay. Something was going on in Isabella's life that did not sit well with him.

He pulled her a little closer, and he could feel how thin she'd become. Instead of feeling the curve of her breasts, he felt her ribs.

Instead of feeling the comfort of her curves, he just felt bones. She was a shadow of the woman he'd met at his brother's wedding. Not only physically, but mentally as well.

She was no longer the vivacious woman he'd met and become very fond of. This woman was withdrawn. This woman was like a wall-flower. and had lost her personality, almost as though it had been beaten out of her.

He froze. *Is that what happened? Had someone used her as a punching bag?*

"Your plaster is gone," he said, his hand cupping her cheek.

She looked up at him with those big blue eyes. He stroked her blonde hair and he revelled in her closeness "Today," she said. "The plaster came off this morning."

She smiled a tiny tentative smile, then looked down to the floor. He put his fingers under her chin and teased her face toward him once more.

"Isabella," he said breathlessly, then covered her lips with his.

She tasted of coffee and cake. She tasted sweet. She tasted of pure Isabella.

His hands went up her back as their lips met. He rubbed his hands up and down, and in circles. He felt her relax against him, and he smiled.

He was not going to be the reason for this woman's angst, he was going to be the solution for it.

As he kissed her again, he felt the tingle of her lips against his. He felt fairies dancing up and down his spine. And he felt his heart finally melting after all his heartbreak, and after all this time.

* * *

Chase lost all sense of time.

He was lost in the moment. Lost in Isabella's arms. Lost in what could have been. What should have been.

He wanted to wine and dine her. Wanted to take her places, and wanted to let himself fall in love with beautiful Isabella.

Instead he had his deputy on a hunting trip. Metaphorically, not physically, but still a hunting trip.

His arms held tight to the woman standing in his arms. And he savoured every moment.

A light tap at the door brought him back to the present.

He felt Isabella shaking before she stepped back out of his arms. He looked down into her eyes. "It's okay," he said reassuringly. "It will just be one of my staff."

"Enter." He said the words as he indicated for her to sit.

Deputy Chris Dolan entered the room He glanced from Chase to Isabella. "Apologies, Sheriff," the deputy said. "I didn't realise you had company."

He turned to walk away, but the sheriff stopped him. "It's fine, Deputy," Chase said. "I'd like you to meet a friend of mine. Miss Isabella O'Reilly. Isabella, this is Deputy Chris Dolan. He's been with the Sheriff's Office for as long as I can remember."

The shocked expression on the deputy's face told Chase this was a good thing. Now he knew who he was investigating. Now it was personal.

Not that he thought the deputy wouldn't get the job done. He would. Of course he would. He was

35

the ultimate professional. But *knowing* Isabella, *knowing* the victim of the crime, always put another layer on it.

"Miss O'Reilly," Deputy Chris said as he reached for her hand.

Isabella stood as he shook her hand, and Chase watched the shock on the deputy's face as he saw how thin she was. The poor condition she was in.

And she was visibly shaking. All that would help spur the investigation along.

The deputy had seen photographs of the wedding. It was the talk of the town at the time. The deputy's eyes flew to Chase. He would remember the beautiful woman who was Chase's partner at the wedding.

"Isabella was at Rory and Missy's wedding," Chase offered, in case Chris still hadn't put two and two together. "She's Missy's cousin."

Deputy Dolan nodded as realization finally dawned.

"Very pleased to meet you, Ma'am," he said, pushing his hat way back on his head, then suddenly pulling it off.

Chase grinned. That was so much Chris Dolan. Always the gentleman, but he'd apparently been so shocked by Isabella's appearance, all etiquette went out the window.

"Sorry to have disturbed you, Sheriff. I have an update on a case, but it can wait." He stared Chase squarely in the eye, then backed out of the room. "Pleased to have met you, Ma'am."

And without another word he was gone.

"I, I have to go too," Isabella said, suddenly.

Chase frowned at her. "Stay a little longer?" he asked quietly, but Isabella knew if she stayed any longer she'd want to wrap her arms around him again. She'd want him to hold her close once more.

She'd want to feel his lips on hers again, and this time she wouldn't want him to let her go. No, better she break their ties right now.

She had no intention of putting Missy and the rest of the Callahan family in danger. Hell, even Grace could be in the firing line.

She'd known Missy all her life, and Grace for many years now, and the last thing she wanted to do was put the two of them in physical danger. The brothers could look after themselves and their partners, she was certain, but she still didn't want to push the boundaries.

As she stood to leave, she resolved to tell Missy she was leaving as soon as her treatment was finished. That way she would be stronger, and would be able to take care of herself a little better. At least she hoped so.

Chase stepped toward her and pulled her close. "Chase," she said softly. "I have to go." She looked up into his big brown eyes. Eyes that always drew her in. His puppy eyes, she liked to call them.

She fought to hold back tears. She didn't want to leave this wonderful man. She'd finally found the person she believed to be her soul-mate, and now she had to let him go.

For his sake.

Her heart was breaking into little pieces. Shattering her whole life.

"What is this?" he asked, as an errant tear rolled down her cheek.

Isabella brushed at her tears and ran out of the room, leaving Chase staring after her.

* * *

Missy sat patiently outside the Sheriff's Office, waiting for Isabella to return.

She thought about Lizzie's ploy to get them together. She hoped it worked. Chase needed someone to care about, and Isabella needed someone to look out for her, and to love her.

She already knew Chase was falling for Isabella. Correction: had fallen for her.

It didn't take Einstein to work out the two had clicked at the wedding. It was just a shame Isabella had rushed off back to the rodeo.

A few weeks together was probably all it would have taken to get those two to realize they were made for each other.

Missy sighed.

It was very clear something was going on with Isabella, but no one had any idea what. She'd never been this secretive before. Growing up together they always shared secrets with each other. It had always been hard for them to hide anything from the other. They could read each other like a book.

She was very aware that Isabella was in some sort of trouble. Perhaps even in danger. When you do a job as long as her cousin had, you do not injure yourself at work. Not constantly like she'd supposedly been doing lately, anyway.

Missy knew that rodeo inside and out. She knew Isabella's boss. If he thought she was being reckless, or something was causing her to be hurt, he'd fixed it immediately.

She shook her head. No, this was not work related, she was certain.

Isabella had been eerily silent after she'd gone home from the wedding. Missy had barely heard from her, which was strange. They usually kept in touch regularly, but her cousin hadn't answered her letters or her phone calls.

Missy scratched her head. She hoped Chase could get to the bottom of it. Isabella suddenly came running out of the building, and Missy stood, a little panicked. "Are you okay?" she asked. As Isabella got closer she saw the tears, noticed her red eyes.

"I have to leave," she said.

Missy stood in shock. "What do you mean? What did Chase say to you?" she asked, suddenly annoyed at her brother-in-law.

"Chase did nothing," Isabella said. "Except hold me in his arms and kiss me. And make me feel loved."

Missy grinned. Aunt Lizzie might be a schemer, but she knew her stuff.

Suddenly she was confused. "So, Lizzie's ploy worked, but you're upset about it?" She rubbed her hands across her swollen belly.

"No!" Isabella was adamant, then suddenly sat. "Yes and no," she said. "I like Chase, I really do."

"So, what's the problem?" Missy asked, even more confused.

"It's complicated," Isabella said, then hurried back toward Missy's car.

Clearly, she didn't want to talk about it, so there was no point pursuing the subject. Missy didn't want to upset her any more than she already was.

* * *

Missy finished making popcorn, bucket loads of it, and set it on the table. She opened a bottle of wine for Grace and Isabella and found some soda for herself.

She had a box of chocolates, and a handful of movies they could choose from.

Dinner was over, and she was pushing Rory out the door. "Go to Chase and Jordon," she said. "And go over to that hermit of a brother of yours," she told him.

Rory looked shocked. "Who, Kody? He won't play ball," Rory said, scratching his head.

"Yes, Kody. Now go," she said, giving him one last shove.

Grace arrived as Missy put the last-minute touches to the sitting room. Isabella was in the bath, at Missy's insistence. She needed some 'me time' and she got it. Grace was bringing the items for facials, and they were all going to be pampered before they began to watch a movie.

The soppier, the better.

Isabella appeared in the doorway, wrapped in a thick white towel, water dripping down her legs. Her hair fell limp, and she looked worse than she did bone dry.

"I thought I heard your voice," she told Grace. She moved toward her friend and hugged her. "I've missed you," she said, pulling her closer still.

"I missed you too," Grace said pushing away from her. "Let me look at you." She took a long look, and ran her eyes up and down Isabella's length. "You look dreadful, hun. What have you done to yourself?"

Missy gasped. Grace didn't mean to be harsh, she was just being truthful. And perhaps that was what Isabella needed to hear.

"Go and dry yourself off, and come back prepared for fun," Grace told her, smiling.

The smile disappeared the moment Isabella was out of the room. "What the hell happened to her," Grace demanded when her friend was out of earshot.

"I have no idea," Missy said. "She won't say. But one thing is for sure," she blinked, trying to stop her tears. "Chase *will* get to the bottom of it, and make sure she's safe."

"I sure hope so," Grace said, hugging Missy close. "I sure hope so."

By the time Isabella returned, the two women had the room set up for facials. They took turns at giving each other a facial, and they had manicures. Once that was all over, it was time to watch a movie.

The three decided on *You've Got Mail.* Once the movie was over, Isabella sighed. "It would be wonderful to have someone care for you like that," she said.

Missy stared at her. "We care!" she said.

"Yeah, but you're not a man," she bit back.

Missy shook her head. "But Chase is, and he cares," she said. "A lot."

"Does he," Isabella asked. "Really?"

"He sure does. More than you realize."

Missy got up and removed the DVD, ready for the next one.

* * *

Missy stood with three dressmaker's pins sticking out of her mouth. "Stand still," she mumbled as she tried to pin them in the right place.

"Let's face it," Isabella protested. "This dress is way past its best-by date. Chase is not going to be impressed with it, even with your alterations." She looked down at Missy, her eyes filling with tears.

"Right. That's it then." Missy snatched the pins out of her mouth, and helped Isabella off the chair. "We're going into town."

"But...."

"No buts. There's a great boutique in town, and we're going to shop for a new dress. My treat."

Isabella bit back her tears. It had been a long time since anyone, apart from Missy and her extended family, had been kind to her. Life had been difficult since Missy's wedding. And frankly, she realized she should never have left.

Her heart was with Chase. Even though they barely knew each other, she was more and more aware as the days passed, that he was the man for her.

She'd fallen in love with him quickly. Quicker than she'd ever expected.

How can love suddenly appear like that? You know someone only a week or so, and you've fallen hard?

But she knew it could happen. Just look at Missy and Rory. It didn't take long for them to know they'd found their soul-mate.

And that's how it was for Isabella and Chase. At least she hoped it was for Chase. He seemed to be as enamoured with her, as she was with him.

Missy held her hand as she stepped down off the chair. She wiped at her eyes and sighed. Missy always could read her. She always knew what was best for her.

Because they'd grown up together, they could read each other like a well-worn book. She smiled and held Missy's hands. "Thank you. A new dress will be just the ticket."

She hugged her cousin tight, despite the bulging belly between them. As they separated, Isabella rubbed her hands across Missy's belly. "I can't wait for this little fellow to arrive," she said.

Missy stared into her eyes. "Who says it's a fella," she asked. "We have no idea what we're having."

Isabella straightened her shoulders. "Oh, it's a boy alright. I can feel it. A miniature Rory." She smiled and hugged Missy once more.

Chapter Four

Isabella flicked through the dress racks.

As someone who worked in the rodeo, she didn't get to wear dresses often, as she didn't have much time for socializing.

Going on a date was a real treat. Going on a date with Chase was beyond special. It would be the highlight of her year.

Isabella took off her cowgirl hat and ran her hands through her hair. She was so used to wearing a hat, that she couldn't bring herself to take it off.

Even when she wasn't working.

"Over here." Missy called across the shop. Isabella sure hoped she'd found something suitable, because Isabella was having no luck.

"Take a look at this beauty," she said, holding the dress in the air for her cousin to see. "Look at that gorgeous Queen Anne neckline, and the way the skirt flares out. It's really beautiful."

Isabella reached out and touched the pale pink dress. "It's so soft!" She held the dress to her cheek. "Oh my gosh, I think this is it," she said quietly, as she jumped up and down.

Missy grinned at her. "I do too. Now go and try it on."

Isabella headed for the changing rooms while Missy waited outside for her. "How does it look," she heard Missy ask.

Isabella was too busy preening herself in the mirror. "I, I.... this is the one," Isabella whispered. She threw the curtains back and presented herself to her loving cousin.

Missy stared open mouthed, then put her hands to her mouth. "Oh my," she said between her fingers. "If this doesn't knock his socks off, nothing will."

"We'll take it," she said before Isabella could say no. Much to Isabella's dismay, Missy continued looking for more dresses as Isabella returned to the changing rooms.

"Missy, no," she said, taking another dress from Missy's hands and returning it to the rack where it belonged.

"I told you," Missy said. "My treat. Not only do I want you as a friend and cousin, I would love to have you as my sister-in-law too."

Isabella hugged her cousin. "How wonderful would that be?"

Three more dresses were tried and bought before the two women left the store.

* * *

Isabella couldn't contain her excitement.

Chase was taking her on a date. A real date. Where it was just the two of them.

She punched the air and did a little dance in her room. She couldn't wait.

She put on the pale pink dress Missy had bought for her. It was so beautiful, and because it was the right size, it didn't make her look so pale and ill.

She pulled her blonde hair up into a soft bun, and looked at herself in the mirror. A touch of eyeshadow and a lick of lipstick, and she was done.

Missy had taken her to have her hair cut, had bought new clothes for her, as well as their sumptuous girls night in.

She was beginning to feel normal again.

There was a tap at the door. "He's here," Missy said quietly.

Isabella opened the door. "Ta da!" She did a little twirl to show Missy her handiwork. She hadn't felt this happy in ages.

"You look amazing," she said as she hugged her cousin tight. "Chase will be very impressed."

Her heart beat rapidly as they walked into the sitting room where Chase was waiting. She heard his intake of breath, and prayed it was because he liked what he saw, and not the opposite.

He walked toward her, arms outstretched. "You look amazing," he said, wrapping his arms around her, then leaned in to kiss her on lightly on the cheek.

Isabella was disappointed. They'd shared a *real* kiss before. Why not now?

Perhaps he was shy in front of Rory and Missy? Or maybe he thought he'd embarrass her. That would be just like Chase. Always thinking of others.

"We'll catch you later folks," Chase called over his shoulder as they left.

As they settled into Chase's truck, he told Isabella his plans for the evening. "First a movie, then dinner," he said. "If that's okay with you."

Isabella nodded. "Sounds perfectly fine."

"We don't have a movie theatre in River Valley, so we'll have to go to Boulton, about half an hour away."

"Still sounds good."

He looked across at her as he started the truck. He couldn't resist, and leaned in toward her.

Isabella startled. Edged away from him.

"Oh my God, Isabella, I didn't mean to startle you," he said quietly. "Are you alright?" The expression in her eyes told him she wasn't. She was like a deer in headlights. And she was ready to bolt.

49

He watched her closely, her hand on the door, ready to jump out if necessary. It was all starting to make sense now.

Deputy Chris had uncovered some important information, but Chase didn't want to think about that now. He just wanted to give Isabella a night to remember. And that's exactly what he intended to do.

He reached over and touched her hand gently. "Still want to go," he asked. "Because I really want to spend some time with you." He looked deep into her eyes. "Just you and me. Getting to know each other."

She nodded but didn't say a word.

"At the wedding," he said in a whisper. "We didn't have time to learn about each other, but we clicked. At least I thought we did."

He leaned back and let her take it all in. She still didn't say a word. "You are a very special woman, Isabella," he said. "Let me prove it to you."

She took a deep breath. Then another, and another. She spoke so quietly he almost didn't hear her. "And you are very special to me too," she said. She lifted her hand and put it on his. "I dearly want to get to know you. And your family."

She smiled a very tentative smile and he knew she was trying hard. He also knew this was probably one of the hardest things she'd done in a long time.

He had to earn her trust. And earn her trust he would.

"I really like you, Isabella. Perhaps one day we can be more than friends." He took a deep breath. He was torn. Torn between still loving his dead wife Jenny, and wanting to live the rest of his life, perhaps with Isabella.

"This is hard for me," he said. "Did Missy tell you about...."

Isabella looked him right in the eyes. He could see the compassion. She knew.

"About Jenny? Your wife?" She licked her lips. "It must be extremely difficult for you. I'm so sorry."

She said it with passion. He really believed she was sorry. He was sorry. Relived that day over and over. Couldn't get it out of his head.

He wasn't there for her when she needed him. And he couldn't console himself. Couldn't forgive himself, despite being told hundreds of times it wasn't his fault.

If he'd been in the car with her, they'd have both been killed, and he wouldn't constantly go through all this pain. This torture he endured day after day, night after night.

He shook his head, trying to get rid of the memories. Of the vision of his darling wife lying in the morgue after the accident. Having to identify her.

"Chase." She touched him lightly on the arm. "Are you okay?" She whispered the last words, and it was enough to pull him back into reality.

"Yeah," he said quietly. "Just thinking back to that day."

He shuffled in his seat. "Ready to go? It's getting on. Maybe dinner first?" He had to work hard to put himself into the right frame of mind. He wasn't willing to spoil their first date. Isabella deserved to be treated like the princess he knew she was.

"Whatever you like. I'm not fussed."

He'd noticed she didn't eat much lately, and Missy had told him as much. Perhaps tonight he could spoil her and get to indulge herself, although that seemed highly unlikely.

It was worth a try.

* * *

At the restaurant, they were escorted to their table.

It was by the window, facing out over the mountains. In the twilight, it was beautiful. Isabella could only begin to imagine what it would be like in darkness.

The moon was beginning to rise behind the mountains to the east, at the same time the sun was setting to the west. The color of the sky was a sight to behold.

She'd lived near the city most of her life. On the outskirts anyway. She'd never seen a moon so big and so bright. It made her feel melancholy. And bewitched.

She felt emboldened.

Isabella reached across the table and put her hand gently onto Chase's. She softly rubbed her thumb across his palm. Looked at his strong arms, and then looked into his face.

The moonlight was playing in his eyes. It was magical. She knew their night would be magical too.

She really wanted this friendship to go further than just being friends. But there were roadblocks and she didn't know how to get rid of them.

"Chase...." She said, but then changed her mind. Would he run a mile if he knew what she was going through? Or would he try and help her?

She lifted her hand and waved it in the air. "No, don't worry. It's alright," she said under her breath.

He leaned into her. "Tell me," he said. "I won't bite, I promise."

He smiled at her and lit up the room. She felt safe with him, and with every moment she was with him she felt more and more drawn to him.

"I..."

"Your menus, Sir, Madam."

She leaned back. The moment had passed. She couldn't speak now. Besides, she would spoil the whole evening. And Chase deserved a night out. Missy said he never did anything for himself. Worked all sorts of long hours at the Sheriff's Office, even working Sundays.

No. This was not the time.

"Thank you," Chase said abruptly, obviously annoyed at the interruption.

"Would you like tonight's specials, Sir?" The waiter looked uncomfortable, as though he'd picked up on Chase's irritation, and was trying to make amends.

"Sure, thanks."

As the waiter reeled off the night's specials, Isabella closely watched Chase. His face was so beautiful. Not that you're meant to call men beautiful. But he was.

She stared at his nose. His tiny button nose. And those eyes, those brown puppy dog eyes – she could easily get lost in them.

She startled as the waiter leaned over and placed a glass of water in front of her. "Isabella, are you okay?" It was Chase. His hand covered hers, and she felt the gentleness and the warmth it brought to her.

His thumb gently stroked her palm, and she felt less stressed. Much more relaxed. His nearness made her feel comfortable. Made her feel as though anything was possible.

"I apologise, Madam. I did not mean to startle you." The waiter nodded and walked away.

Chase slid his chair close to Isabella. "No reason we can't sit together," he told her. "It's cosier this way."

She smiled at him, reassured by his closeness. His proximity.

* * *

As she perused the menu, Chase saw her look over the top of it at him. It was as though she needed reassurance he was still there. He slid sideways, even further, toward her until their shoulders touched.

She smiled.

He wouldn't move from her side if that's what it took to make her feel comfortable. She had quite obviously been through some sort of trauma, and Chase would ensure he got to the bottom of it, and make her life better.

It killed him to watch her go through this pain. This hell she was enduring. Heck, if it was his Jenny, he'd do everything he could to stop it, and he would do the same for Isabella.

He'd even do it for a stranger.

Isabella had some sort of pull on him. He was enamoured with her, and he couldn't shake her. If he thought about it, he didn't want to anyway.

He was comfortable with her. Felt that pull he hadn't felt for some years.

But he would take things slowly. If Isabella decided she wanted to see him again, that was.

No matter what, he would find out what was going on, and he would deal with it. He owed her that much.

"Are you ready to order yet?" It was that pesky waiter again.

"Isabella?"

"Yes, I'm ready," she said, sounding less than confident, and closed the menu.

* * *

Whether it was the food or the company, Chase didn't know. At first Isabella pushed her food around her plate. Played with her food, almost. He'd mentioned how good the food was, and she tucked right in.

It made him happy, because she sure could do with a good feed. Right now, she was skin and bone.

If it meant he needed to take her out every single night to get her to eat, so be it.

Whatever it took.

After they'd eaten the main course, Isabella was full to the brim, she'd said. So they ordered coffee and decided to have dessert later if they felt like it.

Chase paid the bill, and they walked down the road to the movie theatre. "What would you like to see," he asked, as they arrived in the foyer.

Isabella looked around at the posters, then turned to him. "Whatever you like. I haven't been to a movie in years, so anything is good to me."

Chase bought two tickets to the most recent movie, bought some popcorn, drinks, and chocolates, and they moved inside.

They arrived just in time to see the end of the advertisements, and wandered down the carpeted steps.

The theatre was almost empty so they had a choice of wherever they wanted in the whole place. As they entered, Isabella scrutinized the place. She held tight to Chase's hand as they continued down the steps, and looked up to check out any balconies that might be there.

There weren't any.

He was totally aware of her actions. She was making sure no one could come at her from any angle. These were not the actions of a regular person. He, more than most, knew that.

It reaffirmed his suspicions there was more to Isabella's injuries than she was letting on. For the sake of his sanity, and her happiness, he let it ride.

For now.

"Let's sit here," he said, indicating seats in the middle, about half way down. He didn't say anything to Isabella, but it was most unlikely someone could creep up on her when they were in that spot.

Hell, it was most unlikely someone would creep up on her with him there. He'd be on them in a flash.

He felt his blood boil, and knew for her sake, he had to calm down. This was meant to be a fun night out for them both.

Right now, all he wanted to do was hold her in his arms and make her whole world better. Make her life perfect. Make *their* lives perfect. Together.

As the movie began, the lights began to dim. There were only two other couples in the same theatre. It felt more intimate that way, and Chase liked intimate when he was courting a woman.

Sure, he was all rough and tumble when it came to work. The Sheriff *had* to be like that. He was leader of the gang. He had to make sure people followed orders, and he had to roll with the punches sometimes, but when it came to women, especially women he cared about, it was a totally different ball game.

He glanced across at Isabella in the darkness. Her silhouette beside him made him melancholy.

He surveyed her soft outline. She was pretty. Really pretty. Even despite her massive weight loss.

Was he pretending she was Jenny? Or was he really seeing Isabella for herself?

He shook his head, and closed his eyes. He knew it was Isabella he saw. As much as he had loved Jenny back then, and still loved her now, he needed to move on. As hard as it would be.

He was sure his darling Jenny would understand. She would want him to lead a happy life, and not mope around for the rest of his days.

His brothers had all told him as much, but he wouldn't listen. Now that the right person had come along, it all made perfect sense.

His hand slipped into hers, and he moved his knee across, so their knees touched.

"This is nice," she said, turning her head toward him. Without thinking, he leaned in and kissed her gently. She reached up and touched his cheek with her hand. It was cold from the cup of soda she'd been holding, but he didn't care. Only cared that she had reacted this way. "Really nice," she added.

59

She tasted of soda, and her lips were cold, but again, he didn't care. He only cared that he was here with Isabella. Alone.

At least, almost alone.

And in the dark, no one could see them, so they had time together without interruption. He continued to kiss her, and they missed the start of the movie, but neither of them cared.

The more he held her, the more he wanted her, but he wasn't going to rush it. She was fragile, in more ways than one.

Her hand came down from his cheek, and rested in his hand. "We need to watch the movie," she whispered, and turned her head back toward the giant movie screen.

"Do we have to," he whispered back, a big grin on his face.

As she turned toward him, she must have seen his smile, because she smiled, and looked down into her lap, in a coy sort of way.

Coy suited her, he decided. It was sexy in its own sly way.

They both sat back and enjoyed the movie, their hands still encased in each other's, sipping their drinks, and sharing a giant cup of popcorn.

As the lights came up, Isabella turned to Chase. "That was beautiful," she told him, tears in her eyes.

"What's this then," he asked, wiping the stray tears from her cheeks. "I know some women cry at sad movies, but this one had a happy ending."

"Yes, it did," she said. "Very happy. Some people have all the luck."

Chapter Five

As they wandered out of the theatre, holding hands, Chase had an idea. "Shall we go up the mountain to the lookout," he asked. "Then maybe to Aunt Lizzie's Kitchen for a late-night snack."

"Don't you have to get up early?"

It was just like Isabella to worry about him. Her eyes said yes, but her words said otherwise.

"Don't you worry about me. I'm a big boy, I can look after myself," he said, laughing. "What do you say? It won't take long to drive up there once we're back in River Valley."

She nodded her agreement.

"You'll get to see the whole of River Valley, which isn't a lot. But more than that, you'll get a much better look at that big ol' moon you adored so much at the restaurant."

They moved toward his truck and quickly went on their way.

Isabella hardly said a word on the way up the mountain. But that was okay. Chase left her alone with her thoughts. He was sure she had a lot of stuff rolling around in her mind. Things he wanted to know. Maybe one day she'd trust him enough to tell him.

As they pulled into the look out car park, she started to speak. "Chase, I...." As the truck stopped, she leapt out of the vehicle. "Oh my gosh, this is so beautiful!"

Damn it. Every time she started to tell him something, she was interrupted.

She jumped up and down, and ran over to the rail, taking in the panoramic views. She looked up into the moon, and he saw the joy written all over her face.

She ran to him, and put her arms around him. "Thank you. Thank you so much for bringing me to this gorgeous place!" She hugged him with all her might, and Chase glowed in the simplicity of it all.

He stood there momentarily, his wits had suddenly left him. But then he came to his senses and wrapped his arms around this beautiful woman he'd had the good fortune to spend the evening with.

She looked up into his face as he looked down at her. He brushed a wisp of hair out of her eyes and stared at her for long moments.

"Isabella," he whispered, seconds before his lips descended on hers. Her lips were warm this time, but still tasted of cola.

He gently brushed his lips against hers, running his tongue along her bottom lip, then pulling it into his mouth. He wanted to taste more of her. Get to know her better.

He heard her groan moments before she sank into him. He smiled beneath the kiss. She was feeling more comfortable with him every time they were together.

That made him happy.

More than happy. Ecstatic.

They stood there in the silence. With nothing but the trees and the owls and the mountains surrounding them.

Why then, did Chase suddenly hear a twig snap? As though someone had stood on it. They were out there alone, so it shouldn't happen.

He put a finger to his lips, and shook his head. He didn't want to scare her, but he wanted to be sure.

There it was again.

He leaned in to her and whispered in her ear. "We're going back to the truck. As quickly as you can." He put his fingers under her chin and lifted her eyes to his face. "You okay," he asked quietly.

She didn't speak. Didn't indicate she was scared. Just nodded and did as he asked, and did it quickly.

He locked the passenger side door as he helped her in, then moved to the driver's side as fast as he could. Again, locking the door. All the doors.

64

Chase started the engine, then left the car park without another word.

As he looked in the rear-view mirror, he saw the silhouette of a man standing in the car park.

Chills went down his spine.

When they were far enough away that he felt Isabella was safe, he looked to her. She was shaking, but stony-faced.

"Chase," she said.

But he put up a hand to stop her. "Not now," he said. "Let's make sure we're home-free and *then* we can talk."

It was a bold move to stop her when she was finally ready, but he needed to get them out of there, and out of danger.

* * *

Isabella sat across from Chase at Aunt Lizzie's Kitchen.

It was private, since it was so late, and they were currently the only customers. She was still shaking from the experience on the mountain, but she breathed deeply trying to calm herself.

Chase sat there watching her. Quietly waiting until she was ready.

Lizzie had served their coffees and left them to it. Chase could tell she knew something was wrong, but she didn't mention it.

65

She came back soon after bringing a plateful of petit desserts for them to share.

"Nice to see you out and about, young Chase," she said, smiling broadly. "I see my little gift the other day worked well. Very well indeed."

She scampered off before Chase could answer. He leaned over the table and placed his hand on Isabella's. He could still feel her trembling and knew she would probably be like that for a while after such a scare.

"Tuck in," he said quietly, knowing once she started telling her story it was unlikely she'd feel like eating.

He dished up several of the petit delicacies onto a small plate for her. One thing he loved, and that was Aunt Lizzie's food.

He'd been going to that café for as long as he could remember and wasn't going to stop going any time soon.

He looked over to the woman standing behind the counter. She smiled and gave him a little salute. She'd been trying to hook him up with eligible young woman for the past few years. This time he was happy with her interference.

He smiled back and returned the salute. *Good ol' Aunt Lizzie, she is a kind old bird.*

"They are so yummy!"

Isabella's words interrupted his thoughts, and he was pleased to see she was eating the dessert. He picked a few and placed them on his plate and began to tuck in.

"They so are," he said, shoving yet another dessert in his mouth. "We might have to get seconds." He smiled at her and she chuckled, dropping her eyes in that sexy way she had about her.

Once they'd finished, he asked Lizzie to refill their coffees. He was sure they were both going to need it.

He'd asked his deputy to join them after their supper, which didn't go down well.

"You've been investigating me?" Isabella was annoyed, but it was the least of Chase's worries.

"I had to keep you safe," he said quietly. "And just as well. Look what happened up on the mountain."

She pushed non-existent stray hair back off her face. "I know," she said. "And I'm sorry. So sorry I got you tied up in all this." She stared down into her lap, twisting her hands as she did so.

Deputy Chris Dolan pulled out his notebook, and began to act very official. "If you don't mind me asking, Ma'am," he said. "When did this all start?" He had his pen poised, ready to write notes.

"After I went back home after the wedding." Isabella squared her shoulders and sat way back in her chair. "I really fell for Chase and wanted to get him out of my head. I had to work anyway, so did the best thing I could." She licked her lips. "I went home and found myself a boyfriend."

Chase looked up sharply and stared at her for a few moments.

"As it turned out, it wasn't a good move," she said. "He seemed nice on the surface, but deep down he was quite violent."

Chris looked to Chase. "That's pretty much what I was able to find out too," he said, addressing Chase.

"I rang your boss," Chase said. "I knew they weren't work injuries."

Isabella started to stand, but he grabbed her hand. "Please stay," he said softly. "This is not about victim-blaming. It's about catching the mongrel who is doing these things to you. Correction. *Was* doing these things. It will never happen again, I promise you."

He could see the tears trying to break through, and could see Isabella was doing her best to stop them. She sat down slowly and bowed her head, so he couldn't see her face.

"Isabella." She ignored him at first, so he repeated his plea. "Isabella." This time it was almost a whisper. He put his fingers to her chin and teased her face to look to him. "You are very special to me,

68

and I am going to help you. No matter what, I'm going to get this guy."

A chill suddenly went up his spine.

"He's out there now, watching us. I can feel it," he said as he stood.

Chase and the Deputy strode to the front door. They stood outside the café and looked around. "I can feel him there too," Chris said, his voice lowered. "You want me to go search?"

Chase looked at him in the dulled light. "I don't think so. We don't know what we're up against here. And this bastard is obviously violent."

Chris nodded, and the two returned inside.

Isabella was sipping on her coffee when the pair sat down. "Did you see him?" Chase was sure she didn't really want to know, but felt compelled to ask.

He shook his head.

"We'll stay here a bit longer," he said. "Then we're going back to my place for the night." He grinned at her. "You are now officially in my protective custody."

* * *

Isabella didn't know what to say, so she didn't say a word.

Until they arrived at Chase's place.

He had a lovely home. Modern looking from the outside, with a porch running all the way around. Ranch house style, Missy called it.

Inside it was roomy, but cosy at the same time. The sitting room was filled with comfortable chairs, low tables, and a large screen television. Did he ever watch it? She understood his work was his life.

The kitchen was fairly large too. Bigger than you'd expect for a home with two people in it. She knew Jenny enjoyed baking, so perhaps it had been custom-built with her in mind.

Chase had told her to wander around and make herself comfortable. She'd felt more than comfortable the moment she walked in the door.

The house was welcoming, and she felt as thought she'd lived there for many years. There were three bedrooms, Chase's room being the biggest, with an ensuite going off it.

It was reasonably bare, and it was obvious it was a man's room. He was tidy, as she'd suspected he would be. There were no clothes laying on chairs or the floor, and the king size bed was made.

He walked up behind her as she stood in the doorway and surveyed it. He wrapped his arms around her, and Isabella sank into him. She closed her eyes and enjoyed being in his arms again. Being with him again. Being held and comforted by him again.

She could very easily get used to this.

He leaned forward and gave her a quick kiss on the bare neck. "Kettle's on if you'd like a cuppa," he said, as he pushed her gently forward into the large room.

She shook her head. She'd had more than enough coffee tonight. As it was she worried she wouldn't sleep – between the coffee and the threats.

"It's nice," she told him, and really meant it. She could easily get used to sleeping there. But she mustn't think such things. Mustn't be presumptuous.

How she would love to be part of Chase's life, but not unless he wanted her to be.

"This is the larger of the spare rooms," he said as they moved along the passageway. "It's right next to my room, so you'll be safe here." He put his hand on her shoulder to reassure her, and she shivered.

His touch was enough to start her longing all over again. Longing to be in his arms. Longing for his kiss. Longing for Chase.

"You're shaking," he told her, and until that moment she didn't realize she was. He pulled her to him, and wrapped his arms around her. This time they were face to face. "You *will* be safe here, Isabella," he said, his words whispered in her ear. "I promise with all my heart. I will not let anyone hurt you." He leaned down and lightly kissed her on the lips.

She stared into his face. His eyes twinkled in the fluorescent light, and lit up. Their glances held for some minutes, and no words were spoken. He was there for her, and that was all that mattered right now.

Everything else could come later.

If that was what Chase wanted. He had his own demons to exorcise. Like the memory of his dead wife.

Isabella knew it must be hard for him. Having to choose between her and his wife. A wife he would still be with today if it wasn't for a drunk driver.

"I, I'm sorry," she said. "Sorry for everything." And she was. Sorry she'd interrupted his life, sorry she'd let things get so out of hand. But most of all she was sorry she'd ever left River Valley.

Things could have been so different between them if she'd stayed. But she'd had a job to return to. Things she had to do. Little did she know her entire life would change because of a chance meeting with a man she'd never met before. A man who had a hidden violent streak.

A man who had nearly killed her on more than one occasion.

She shuddered.

She was safe now, and she needed to remember that.

"Oh," she said, suddenly remembering. "I don't have any clothes with me. No nightgown. Nothing."

Chase smiled down at her. "Nothing sounds good," he said, grinning from ear to ear. He lifted his hand to her cheek. "I'm sure I can find a t-shirt for you to wear to bed," he said. "But it will probably swim on you."

She laughed. "Yes, it probably will."

* * *

Isabella decided to have a cup of tea before bed. To calm her nerves.

She had already donned Chase's oversized t-shirt, and it certainly was big. It was nearly down to her ankles. He was such a tall man at 6'4" — especially compared to her petite 5'5". Perhaps that was one of the reasons she felt so safe with him.

She shook that thought out of her mind. It was simply because it was Chase. When you loved someone as much as she loved Chase, you immediately felt safe with them nearby.

She gazed at him over the brim of her cup. The hot liquid soothing as she sipped.

"Chase," she said. "I don't want to put you in any danger." She took a deep breath. "Perhaps you should just take me to a motel." She put her cup down on the table.

"What the hell....?" He scowled. She didn't like it when he scowled. "I've got deputies outside patrolling the place. You're safe here. Don't stress." He reached over and put his hand over hers. His thumb stroking her hand lulled her into feeling better about the whole situation.

"You have?"

"I sure have," he said. "You are totally safe." He stared at her for a long moment then grinned. "You can sleep in my bed if it makes you feel safer," he said, chuckling as he did.

"Oh sure," she said. "You'd love that wouldn't you?" She grinned, knowing he was joking, but deep down she wouldn't say no if she thought he was being serious.

* * *

Despite thinking it would be to the contrary, Isabella fell asleep almost the moment her head hit the pillow.

She dreamed of being chased, and hurt. Unconsciously, she rubbed her recently broken wrist.

She tossed and turned throughout the night, and every time she awoke, listened for any out of place sounds. She'd heard none.

She sighed and tried to sleep again. She looked across at the clock. It was 4.30am. She could hear the birds twittering, and frogs croaking. Trees

74

moved in the breeze, and she could hear water flowing.

Chase had told her a stream ran through his property, so that would explain the water sound.

It all gave her the jitters. She didn't want to stay here alone for another moment.

She threw back the covers and leapt out of bed, heading for Chase's room. When she opened the door, there he was. Sitting outside her door, looking as innocent as possible.

"What the hell, Chase?" She knew she sounded annoyed, and that was fine. She was annoyed. Nothing had happened. No one had broken in, she was safe.

He sat there and grinned at her, in a way that only Chase could do – and get away with it.

"Whatsup?" There was that grin again.

She ran back to the bed and grabbed her pillow, then attacked him with it. "Hey, ycu're attacking the Sheriff, you know," he said, laughing. "I could arrest you." He still laughed, and she finally stopped when he pulled the pillow out of her hands.

Then the mood changed. He stood up and looked down at her. His eyes smouldering. He was breathing heavily. "Isabella," he said, his voice husky.

Then he pulled her to him.

She stared into his eyes and moved closer to him. Closer so she could feel his heartbeat, closer so he could pull her tight, and closer so her could kiss her senseless.

He slowly bent his head but didn't kiss her. He lingered slightly above them, perhaps waiting for her acceptance.

"Chase, kiss me for goodness sake," she said in a whisper. He gently swiped his lips across hers.

Her mouth tingled. She lifted a hand to them. "Chase," she said breathlessly. "I,"

His fingers touched her cheek. His thumb stroking, and his eyes sizzling. He put a finger to her lips. "Shhhh," he said. And kissed her gently again.

Isabella startled as his phone rang.

"Callahan." His eyes never left her, but he listened carefully to the caller. "Uh huh. Yep. Okay. Thanks."

He didn't say a word, but grabbed Isabella by the hand and pulled her into the bedroom. "Get dressed," he said. "And quickly." He didn't want his deputies ogling her in his oversized t-shirt, with nothing underneath. He smiled inwardly. That privilege was reserved only for him.

He stood there, towering above her, not giving anything away. He didn't want to scare her more than necessary.

"Why," she demanded. But he didn't answer. "Then at least turn around," she said, thoroughly annoyed.

Chase turned, a scowl on his face and his arms across his chest.

"He's out there, isn't he?" She said it matter-of-factly, but Chase knew she would be scared. As she should be.

"Yeah," he said. Not giving too much away. She didn't need to know the mongrel was practically at the front door. He would have been there all night, but in the pitch-black darkness, he wouldn't have been spotted by the deputies. Wouldn't have been able to move around because he couldn't see what he was doing.

Now there was a little daylight, things had changed.

His phone rang again. "Callahan." He took a deep breath. "Yeah, thanks Kody, I know. I have deputies out there," he said. "But thanks, Bro. Appreciated." His brother Kody had seen the stranger from his front paddock as he worked, and so had called Chase.

He disconnected the call. Being a rancher, Kody was always up with the birds.

"Okay, Chase. You can turn around now," Isabella said.

77

Since she had no spare clothes with her, she was in that same pretty dress she wore last night. With those same pretty pink shoes she'd matched to the dress, but this time she had dark circles under her eyes. They marred her beautiful face.

She took a deep breath and looked him square in the eye. "So what now?"

Chase grabbed her by the hand. "We wait." He pulled her toward the sitting room and sat her down. "I'll put the kettle on," he said.

He filled it with water and switched on the appliance. He pulled up the blind in the kitchen and surveyed the area as best he could from within the house.

He had some gall, that was for sure. Chase saw him moving around, trying to hide behind the lavender bushes Jenny had so lovingly planted. The bastard.

He picked up his cell and called Deputy Chris. "He's near the kitchen," Chase said. "Hiding in the lavender bushes. Let's hope he gets stung by the bees," he added, without mirth.

As he watched on, three deputies descended on the area Chase had told them about. He carefully watched as the deputies crept up and all pounced on him at once. After a small scuffle, they eventually handcuffed the man.

He smiled, then turned and went into the sitting room where Isabella was waiting.

"It's over," he said, squatting down to Isabella's sitting level. "We have him in custody."

She leapt forward and hugged him, tears rolling down her face. He knew how she felt. His relief was palpable.

Epilogue

It had been three months since Isabella's ex had been captured and charged.

He was now sitting in a jail cell for his crimes.

Isabella had slowly put back the weight she'd lost, having been fattened up by Missy and Rory, as well as Chase.

Tonight was special. It was to be a Callahan family party, essentially to celebrate the upcoming birth of the newest Callahan.

As the water ran over her long blonde hair, Isabella savoured the warmth surrounding her. Her lavender soap made her skin feel nice, and left her smelling of the lavender bushes Chase loved so much.

She'd all but moved in with Chase, and they were incredibly happy together. So perfect for each other.

After her ordeal, they'd grown even closer, and she didn't complain.

She'd quit her job, and Chase had helped her to bring her belongings to River Valley. Little that they were.

She heard the bathroom door open a slit. "It's nearly time to go," he shouted over the sound of the water.

She looked across to him. "Pass me that towel, will you," she said, teasing him. He apparently didn't need a second invitation because he was there in a flash.

His eyes slid over every inch of her, devouring every nook and cranny.

She stepped out of the shower, and into the towel he held open for her. Chase wrapped the towel around her, and then wrapped her in his arms.

He leaned forward and kissed her bare neck. She groaned. "Chase," she whispered. "I thought we had to go."

"I guess we'll be a little late," he said quietly, his lips covering hers.

* * *

The party was in full swing when they arrived.

"Oh, finally. We thought you'd never arrive." Rory was laughing as he said it, as though he guessed what they'd been up to. Isabella felt the color creep up her face.

Missy sat in a comfortable chair, up front where the action was, only a matter of weeks to go before the littlest Callahan's arrival was due. Isabella walked over and hugged her precious cousin. "Love you," she whispered in Missy's ear.

"Love you too," Missy whispered back.

Isabella sat down next to her, and the two talked. Chase stood chatting with his brothers, then nodded toward Isabella.

"He's up to something," Isabella said. "I have no idea what, but he has been hiding something for days."

Missy smiled. "You know, don't you," Isabella demanded, then pouted. "Not fair." She stomped her foot in a faux tantrum.

Suddenly all sound ceased. The music stopped, the talking stopped, and the whole place was silent.

Chase stood out the front and stared at her. "Isabella," he said quietly. "Can you come here, my darling?" He put his hands out but she sat glued where she was.

She looked him up and down. He was so handsome. So loving. And she thanked her lucky stars for the day she met him.

Missy leaned toward her and whispered in her ear. "Go on," she said. "It will be worth your while." She sat grinning, which only made Isabella more irritated. It seemed everyone knew what was going on except her.

"Isabella," he repeated, but this time he came forward and took her hands. She was now shaking. *What was he up to?*

He escorted her to the front of the room. All eyes were on her. She licked her lips and flicked back an imaginary stray piece of hair.

As she surveyed the crowd, she saw Aunt Lizzie was there. She'd be catering for the night. She often did that for the Callahan family.

Lizzie was grinning from ear to ear. Isabella stared her down, wondering what Lizzie knew, but the other woman continued to grin.

"Isabella," he repeated her name once more, then dropped to the ground. "Isabella, will you marry me?"

Her eyes filled with tears, happy tears, and everyone stood in silence, waiting on her answer, and Isabella was left standing alone as Chase continued to kneel in front of her.

She stared down at him and licked her lips. "Yes," she said quietly. Almost so quiet she didn't know if he would hear. "Yes!" She said it again, more loudly this time.

As he stood, she wrapped her arms around him and hugged him tight. She was never again going to leave her beautiful cowboy Sheriff. She loved him with all her heart.

The End.

About the Author

Multi-published, award-winning author, Cheryl Wright, former secretary, debt collector, account manager, writing coach, and shopping tour hostess, loves reading.

She writes both contemporary and historical western romance, as well as romantic suspense and contemporary romance.

She lives in Melbourne, Australia, and is married with two adult children and has six grandchildren.

When she's not writing, she can be found in her craft room making greeting cards, or in her kitchen baking.

Check out Cheryl's Amazon page –

https://www.amazon.com/author/cherylwright

for a full list of her other books.

Other Links:

http://cheryl-wright.com

https://www.facebook.com/cherylwrightauthor

Join my newsletter

http://cheryl-wright.com/newsletter.html

www.ingramcontent.com/pod-product-compliance
Lightning Source LLC
Chambersburg PA
CBHW071542100726
47908CB00004B/1468